PET SQUAD

PAUL SHIPTON

Illustrated by Jan McCafferty

Oxford University Press 1995

Oxford University Press, Walton Street, Oxford OX2 6DP

Oxford New York
Athens Auckland Bangkok Bombay
Calcutta Cape Town Dar es Salaam Delhi
Florence Hong Kong Istanbul Karachi
Kuala Lumpur Madras Madrid Melbourne
Mexico City Nairobi Paris Singapore
Taipei Tokyo Toronto

and associated companies in
Berlin Ibadan

Oxford is a trade mark of Oxford University Press

First published 1995

ISBN 0 19 916876 8

Printed in Great Britain by
St Edmundsbury Press Limited, Bury St Edmunds, Suffolk

Illustrations by Jan McCafferty

INTRODUCING

The Pet Squad

Mrs Popplewell is my owner. That's her, watching television as usual. Sometimes she watches me swim around and around this bowl. She thinks I'm just a normal goldfish.

Big mistake. My name is Bubbles, and I'm leader of Pet Squad.

Our job is to fight crime and help all animals in need. The other members of Pet Squad are …

Squawk! Pretty Polly! Give us a kiss! (Sorry – can't talk now. My owner's listening. He thinks this is all I can say.)

We're proof that even cats and dogs can get on with each other. Right, Carla?

CARLA

That's right, Pedro.
(And if you believe that, you'll believe anything!)

MIPSY and MUPSY

Being in Pet Squad is a lovely job.

LIGHTNING THE TORTOISE

Don't worry about me – I live up to my name. It may have taken me three hours to get across this garden, but when the Squad needs me I can get my skates on, you'll see.

Together we're the PET SQUAD!

2

The story begins

It was a sunny afternoon, but that didn't stop Mrs Popplewell from staying in and watching television. And they say goldfish lead boring lives!

I just swam laps. There isn't much else to do in a goldfish bowl. At least my bowl is on the window ledge, so I get a good view of what's going on outside.

I swam and waited, swam and waited. In this job you always have to be ready – you never know when you'll be needed.

I didn't have to wait long. Tiddles jumped up onto the ledge outside my window. She's the tabby cat from Number 17. She usually acts cool as ice – the way cats do – but not today. She was flustered and out of breath.

She said the word 'dogs' as if she was spitting out a fish bone.

I nodded and blew a bubble or two. It was the same old problem. A gang of dogs had just moved into the area. They had begun to terrorise everyone, chasing and bullying all the smaller animals.

Their names were Butch, Spud and – worst of all – Blood. Blood was the leader, and he was the biggest, meanest-looking dog I had ever seen.

(Ginger is the kitten from two streets down – a nice kid.)

With the swish of a tail, Tiddles was gone. It was time to give the signal. I swam round and round, faster and faster, until I built up enough speed. Then I jumped out of the water –

That should do it. Now it was up to Polly.

She'll tell you what she had to do.

3

The call goes out

I was sitting on my perch when I saw Bubbles' signal. He jumped out of his bowl twice – that meant it was serious. It was time to call the Squad.

First I had to get past Mr Marshall, my owner. He was sitting in his chair reading the newspaper. He notices if I sneak away because he likes to listen to me.

I edged along the perch and hopped onto the table where he keeps his hi-fi. Slowly I reached out a claw and pressed PLAY on the cassette recorder.

It was Bubbles' idea to make the tape. (He's a genius, you know.) We recorded it one day when Mr Marshall was at work. Now whenever the Squad needs me, I can click on the tape and Mr Marshall doesn't notice I have gone.

Freedom! It felt great to be outside again. I stretched my wings and zoomed upwards into the sky. This was where I belonged.

Of course I didn't forget why I was there. Bubbles had given the signal – it was my job to pass it on to the others.

I swooped over the houses and gardens calling the Pet Squad into action.

That should be enough. It was time to collect Bubbles.

He'll tell you what happened next.

4

The Squad gets together

Once I'd given Polly the signal, I had to wait.

Life isn't easy when you're a goldfish. Try living in a tiny bowl yourself sometime. You can't just nip out whenever you feel like it. But there is always a way round every problem.

Polly arrived. She slipped through the open window and hopped down next to my bowl. Mrs Popplewell was fast asleep – no problem there.

Polly pulled out the plastic bag that was hidden behind the clock. She filled it with water from my bowl, then held it open.

I jumped into the bag, and Polly gathered it up in her beak.

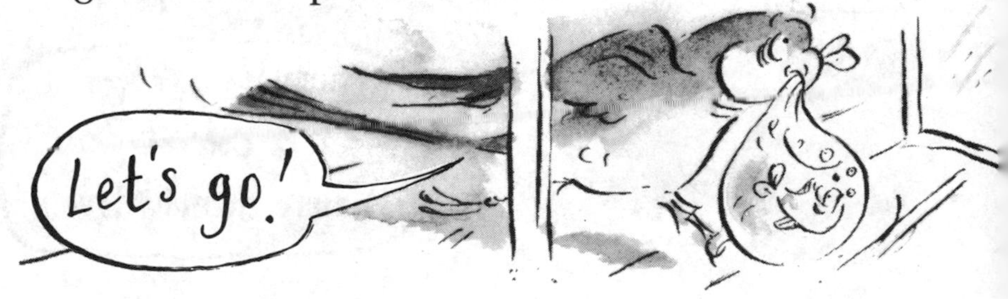

It's not the most comfortable way to travel, but it works for me.

When we got to the meeting place, Carla and Pedro were already there. They were chatting away.

You'd never think they were good friends.

The rabbit twins, Mipsy and Mupsy, were the next to come.

They may look sweet and fluffy, but the twins know how to look after themselves.

Lightning was last to arrive.

The whole Squad was here. Now all we needed was a plan of attack.

'Okay, I'll keep it short,' I said.

I had to. There was only about twenty minutes' worth of water in the plastic bag. After that, it's bye–bye Bubbles.

This was the plan ...

But Pedro will tell you about it.

5

Pedro

Bubbles' plan was brilliant. No surprise there – he's a smart little fish. That's why he's our leader.

He told each of us what we had to do.

But I was still worried. We'd never met anything as dangerous as Blood and his gang before. Every dog for miles around was scared of them. Most of all we were scared of Blood. He was trouble – big trouble.

Just then a little black and white head popped up over the fence.

It was Peachie, the new puppy from down the street. Ever since she had moved to the area, she'd talked about nothing but joining the Pet Squad.

Of course, I had to put Carla in her place.

It was Bubbles who took care of the situation.

Peachie looked as if she had just lost her favourite marrow-bone.

'Don't worry, Peachie,' I whispered as we set off. 'He's only doing it for your own good. Just go home, will you?'

'All right, I suppose so,' said Peachie.

I couldn't quite put my paw on it, but somehow I didn't believe her.

Bubbles will tell you what happened next.

6

The Plan

It was going to be dangerous, but the Squad knew what they had to do. Everyone went off to put the plan into action. Pedro picked me up and carried me to meet the enemy.

We could hear the three dogs before we saw them. There was a chorus of angry barks. And in the middle of it we could hear the frightened cry of Ginger the kitten, stuck up the tree.

'Not all us dogs are like that,' whispered Pedro.

'I know,' I said. 'Now let me do the talking.'

We turned the corner, and there they were – looking bigger and tougher than ever. I knew Pedro was scared – the plastic bag shook in his jaws – but of course he didn't let on. We went closer.

The three dogs sneered when they saw us.

I didn't expect anything more from Butch and Spud. They were mean and dim. But Blood ... he was different. A terrible grin spread across his face. I could see his teeth. They were big.

He edged closer. Spud and Butch followed. I had been wrong: Blood's teeth weren't big, they were ENORMOUS.

I didn't answer. Instead I shouted up Ginger.

Just at that moment, a voice rang out from the next street. The plan had started.

Butch! Here boy! Walkies! Come on boy!

But Polly will tell you all about her part of the plan.

7

Butch goes for a run

Butch's ears pricked up as if they were on springs.

'Wait!' snapped Blood, but it was too late. Butch had been trained always to do what his human master wanted. He raced off in the direction of the voice.

Butch wasn't a good, clever dog. But he WAS a greedy dog and he knew that his master was the person who gave him things like chocolate biscuits.

And so Butch ran and ran after his master's voice.

But something was wrong. Every time Butch reached the place he thought the voice was coming from, it shouted out again from a new place.

Come on, boy! I've got a choccie biscuit for you!

Butch set off again. He was panting hard, and hanging his tongue out in that yucky way dogs do, but he did not stop.

He never guessed who was really shouting at him.

I'm good with voices.

After a few miles, I decided that Butch needed a rest. I flew over to a van parked outside the grocer's shop.

Butch did not stop to wonder why his master was sitting in the back of a delivery van. He ran up and sprang into the back of the van. I slipped out smartly.

The driver had finished unloading his delivery to the shop. Before Butch could let out a bark, the driver had closed the back doors of the van.

Then he got in the driver's seat, turned on the radio, and drove off … with Butch still in the back.

I knew that the van was going to a shop in the next town ... ten miles away.

Butch would have a long walk home before he got any chocolate biscuits.

Part one of the plan had worked like a dream. But what was happening to part two?

Carla will tell you.

8

Spud has a go

Most dogs are okay really. (But don't let Pedro know I said that.) They're just a bit too eager to please humans, that's all.

But mean dogs like Butch and Spud, they're different. They need to be taught a lesson. Pet Squad was going to do just that.

I watched Bubbles and Blood talking, from a safe distance. Part two of the plan was about to begin.

Just then something sped by. It looked like a jet-powered rock. It wasn't. It was Lightning the tortoise on his roller-skate. The message on his shell was painted in bright yellow.

When he read it, Spud howled with rage.

He began to charge after the speeding tortoise.

'Wait!' cried Blood. Again he was too late. Spud had gone.

Now it was time for me to act. I ran to the corner of the High Street – near where Mr Grundy, the lollipop man, helps people across the road. (No one knows why someone as bad-tempered as Mr Grundy became a lollipop man. Who can tell with humans?)

I waited.

First came Lightning. He hurtled round the corner like a low-flying cannonball. He hit a crack in the pavement, and flew up into the air. He sailed over the fence to safety. He had done his bit – now it was my turn …

Spud arrived. He had tried to take a short–cut through a garden, but Lightning had been too fast for him. The dog was puffing and panting hard.

I smiled at the dog's stupidity.

Spud's mean little eyes fell upon me, and I knew his anger was even stronger than his tiredness. He snarled and ran towards me, jaws snapping.

This called for perfect timing.

Spud was picking up speed now, racing across the grass towards me.

I smiled and licked a paw.

The dog's mouth was wide open, teeth bared. He was running faster and faster, his beady eyes fixed on me, a low growl in his throat.

I flicked my tail calmly . . .

Spud sprang forward for the kill, flying through the air. The low growl was now a savage roar …

At the very last second I leapt smartly to one side. It was too late for Spud to stop. He sank his teeth right into Mr Grundy's bottom.

The cry was loud enough to be heard for miles. The lollipop man whirled around.

'You stupid dog!' he yelled, and he took a swing at Spud with his lollipop. Spud dodged, and pelted off down the street. Mr Grundy took off after him, waving his lollipop like a lethal weapon.

I just hoped the others had got on as well as we had.

But I will hand you over to Bubbles. He'll tell you.

9

Bubbles in trouble

I knew that the others would do their best. Now it was my turn. It was time for part three of the plan.

I smiled and stared at Blood coldly.

Blood charged.

Pedro turned and ran. I knew Blood was chasing us. I couldn't see him, but I could hear the scratch of his claws on the pavement.

We didn't have much time. Blood was much faster than Pedro and it didn't help that the little dog had to carry me in his jaws. But he ran for all he was worth.

He pushed his way through a hole in the fence at Number 23. That gave us a few seconds – Blood was too big to fit through the hole. He had to go round.

Pedro whizzed round the corner, past some workmen, and along the row of back gardens.

I could hear Blood close behind, but we only had a few metres to go. Nearly there – Number 17, Number 15, Number 13. At last we reached the garden outside Number 11, where the twins were waiting.

Pedro stopped, and whirled around to face Blood.

At the same instant Mipsy the rabbit popped up from a flower bed in the garden. She held a hosepipe, and it was pointed at Blood. In the background Mupsy stood ready at the tap.

Everyone knows that dogs are scared of being given a bath. We had won!

But something was wrong.

Blood didn't look the least bit worried. In fact, he was smirking.

I didn't like the sound of this.

It was true! Mupsy turned the tap on, but nothing happened. Not a single drop of water came out of the hosepipe.

The big dog came closer still. His growl sent a chill of fear through me.

10

A surprise for Blood

We were in big trouble. Blood took a step towards us. He was enjoying himself.

There was nowhere for Pedro to run, and nothing the twins could do. Blood's huge jaws opened.

But then a cry rang out.

STOP!

It was Peachie, the black and white puppy who had wanted to join Pet Squad. And she wasn't alone.

It looked as if every animal in the area was with her. Dogs of all sizes rubbed shoulders with cats.

Hamsters marched with gerbils, guinea pigs mingled with bunnies. Waves of mice scurried across the pavement. An airborne squadron of budgies flew overhead. It was an animal army! I saw that Ginger the kitten was there too, safely down from the tree.

Blood wasn't stupid. He couldn't fight so many animals, and he knew it. He had lost.

He began to sing a different tune.

The Dog Star is special to all dogs. Swearing on it is the most important thing a dog can do.

Blood swore on the Dog Star.

The cheer from all the animals there was almost loud enough to wake old Mrs Popplewell.

But not quite.

But now I will hand you over to Mupsy. She wanted to have the last word.

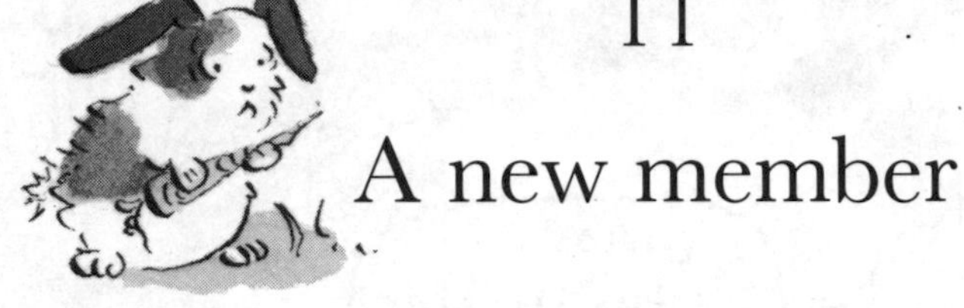

11

A new member

Mipsy and I love a nice party, and it was just as lovely as we had hoped. The whole Squad turned out for the swearing in of a new member.

Because of her quick thinking yesterday afternoon, we are pleased to make Peachie a special member of the Pet Squad. Peachie, please come up to the bowl.

The puppy's tail wagged nervously.

Peachie, do you promise to fight for the rights of the underdog, the undercat, and the underbunny and all other pets in danger?
I do.
Do you promise to keep the Pet Squad motto?
I do.
What is it?
Don't you know? No one hurts an animal and gets away with it.
Oh!

Peachie looked so proud we thought she might explode.

And then Bubbles the goldfish smiled. It's the first time we've ever seen him do that, which is a pity because he's got a lovely smile.

For a goldfish.

* This advert is for animals only.

About the author

When I was growing up in Manchester, I always wanted to be an astronaut, a footballer, or (if those didn't work out for any reason) perhaps a rock star. So it came as something of a shock when I became first a teacher and then an editor of educational books.

I have lived in Cambridge, Aylesbury, Oxford and Istanbul. I'm still on the run and now live in Chicago with my wife Vicky and daughter Megan.

Most of the characters in this book are animals that I have known at one time or another.

Other books at Stages 12, 13, and 14 include:

Billy's Luck by Paul Shipton
Cool Clive by Michaela Morgan
Call 999! by Sylvia Moody
Front Page Story by Roger Stevens
Sing for your Supper by Nick Warburton

Also available in packs

Stages 12/13/14 pack	0 19 916879 2
Stages 12/13/14 class pack	0 19 916880 6